Superstar Sensation!

Grosset & Dunlap • New York

www.bratzpack.com

TM & © MGA Entertainment, Inc. Bratz and all related logos, names and distinctive likenesses are the exclusive property of MGA Entertainment, Inc. All Rights Reserved.

Used under license by Penguin Young Readers Group. Published in 2005 by Grosset & Dunlap, a division of Penguin Young Readers Group, 345 Hudson Street, New York, New York 10014. GROSSET & DUNLAP is a trademark of Penguin Group (USA) Inc. Printed in the U.S.A.

Library of Congress Cataloging-in-Publication Data

Superstar sensation!
    p. cm.
"Bratz and Boyz."
Summary: The Bratz girls and the Bratz boyz join forces in a singing competition at school.
ISBN 0-448-43729-5 (pbk.)
[1. Singing—Fiction. 2. Contests—Fiction. 3. Schools—Fiction.]
PZ7.S6176 2005
[Fic]—dc22
                                            2004012490

ISBN 0-448-43729-5   10 9 8 7 6 5 4 3 2 1

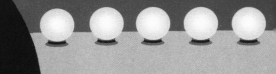

One morning while cruisin' down the hallway on their way to class, Cloe™ and Cade™ saw a poster. "Win a $500 CD Shoppin' Spree gift certificate!" Cade said, stopping suddenly.

"That's a lot of tunes! Let's check it out!" said Cloe.

One night only!!

THE ANNUAL STILES HIGH

Talent Show

THE HIPPEST ACT WINS!

AT THE STILES HIGH AUDITORIUM,
ONE MONTH FROM SATURDAY.

Don't miss out on your
chance to be a star!!

"I can't wait to tell Cameron™, Eitan™, Dylan™, and Koby™," said Cade. "We're totally gonna win this thing— we're the most rockin' guys in the school." He turned to Cloe and added, "Maybe you and your girls can help us."

"Bring it on," said Cade with a grin. "The battle has begun!"

"I don't think that's gonna happen," Cloe said with a laugh. "I have a feeling we girls will be entering, too. You guys may be cool, but you can't compete with real style. When the judges see us onstage, you can bet that we'll win that gift certificate!"

All through English class, Cloe couldn't stop thinking about the competition.

Now's my chance to sing for everyone, she thought. Cloe loved to sing, and she knew she had one choice voice! But no one else had ever heard her, not even her BFFs Jade™, Sasha™, and Yasmin™.

When I mention the talent show, I'll tell them how much I like singing, she thought. *I'd love to be lead!*

As soon as the bell rang, Cloe and Cade ran out of the classroom. It was finally lunchtime and they couldn't wait to tell their friends about the talent show.

When she arrived at the table, Cloe was surprised to discover that her friends already knew about the talent show.

"I'd like to be the lead singer," Cloe heard Sasha say as she reached the lunch table.

Oh, no, Cloe thought. *I've missed my chance!*

"I think that's a great idea, Bunny Boo," Yasmin told Sasha. "Cloe and Jade, what do you think?"

"Sounds good to me," said Jade. "Sasha will have the audience dancing in the aisles with her fresh style."

"I agree," said Cloe. She was a little disappointed that she would not be lead singer, but she wouldn't want to hurt her friend. *It's still gonna be a total blast*, she thought.

"Girls, this is gonna rock!" exclaimed Sasha.

"We're gonna have so much fun!" said Yasmin. "We can pick a song from my karaoke machine!"

"Cool," said Sasha. "And you girls will be up there singing with me, right?"

"Def!" said Cloe, happy to get a chance to sing. "We could be The Backup Bettys!"

"Awesome," said Yasmin. "Count me in!"

I really wanted to design some kickin' costumes, thought Jade. *I won't have time to design them if I'll be singing, too. But if my girl, Sasha, needs me, I'll be there!*

"I'm in, too," said Jade.

"Great!" exclaimed Sasha. "We're gonna have the most slammin' act in the school!"

A few tables away, Cade was trying to convince Eitan, Cameron, Koby, and Dylan that the competition would be a totally kickin' experience.

"It's a great prize, Cade," said Cameron. "But there's no way we can win. None of us can sing!"

"When you've got the musical skills, singing isn't that important!" Cade replied.

"Yeah, Cade's right," said Eitan. "As long as someone can carry a tune, we'll be fine. I'll play the drums. Cade, can you rock out on the guitar for us?"

"You bet," Cade replied. "As long as Cameron will show off his ultra-cool bass skills."

"There'd be no band without them," said Cameron, laughing. "But if we're gonna win, we'll need the best keyboard player in the school." He turned to Koby. "You in?" he asked.

I would so rather put together a mad hot light show with the AV club's high-tech equipment, thought Koby, *but I can't let my boys down.*

"Bring it," said Koby.

"So it looks like that leaves Dylan as our singer," said Cade. "Can you do it, D?"

"Definitely not," Dylan answered, smiling. "But I'll give it a try!"

Since they didn't have much time to get their act together, the girls began rehearsing in the school auditorium the next morning.

"Let's start with the dance sequence that I made up last night," suggested Yasmin.

"Kickin'," said Sasha.

Being awesome dancers, it didn't take the girls long to learn Yasmin's dance.

"Sasha," said Jade, after they had finished a run-through. We're all groovin' dancers, but you shine out there!"

"Thanks, Jade," Sasha replied. "I love to dance."

Next, the girls rehearsed vocals.

"Ready?" Jade asked Sasha after they had warmed up their voices. "When I cue you, start singing. One . . . Two . . . Three . . . Go!"

Halfway through the song, Yasmin turned to Cloe with a worried look on her face.

"What are we going to do, Angel?" she whispered. "Sasha's got the moves, the attitude, and one hot hip-hop style, but she can't hit the high notes!"

Meanwhile, the boys were rehearsing at Dylan's house. They had just finished the song for the first time when Eitan spoke up.

"Okay, guys," he said. "This sounds great, but something's wrong. Did anyone else notice it?"

"Yeah," said Cameron. "Everyone's groovin' on their instruments, and even Dylan's voice sounds just bad enough to be good—"

Everyone laughed.

Cameron continued, "But something's missing."

Koby knew what it was.

"My heart's not in it, guys. I really want to sing with you guys, but the truth is that I'd rather help from backstage. I could design some totally kickin' lighting that would blow the judges away!"

No one said anything. They knew that Koby was right. It wasn't fair to keep him in the band when he felt this way, but they needed a keyboard player, and he was the best.

The girls' rehearsal ended and everyone was packing up. Sasha was feeling a little down, but she didn't have time to dwell. As they were all about to leave, she realized Cloe had disappeared. "Wait up, girls," she yelled. "I'll go find Angel."

As Sasha returned to the auditorium, she heard someone singing. It was Cloe, fixing her hair—and rockin' out to herself!

"Cloe?" Sasha called out.

"Hey, Sash," Cloe replied. "Sorry I'm running a little behind. I'll be right there."

Sasha waited as Cloe finished up. *Wow*, she thought. *I didn't know Cloe was such a slammin' singer. She should be the lead in our group.*

"Thanks for waiting, Sash," Cloe said as they exited the auditorium together. "I didn't mean to take so long."

"It's totally cool, girl," replied Sasha. Then she added, "Listen, Cloe, I heard you singing. You are really groovin'. I think you'd make a much better lead singer for our group. Why didn't you say anything earlier?"

Cloe blushed. She hadn't realized that anyone had heard her.

"I didn't say anything because you seemed to want to sing so badly. I would never get in the way of your dreams," Cloe replied.

"Well, I think you should do it," said Sasha. She knew, with her friend up there, that the girls couldn't lose!

Cloe thought for a moment and then said, "Okay, but only if we add a solo for you. We can't win without your funkalicious singing style!"

That Saturday, the girls arrived at the auditorium for rehearsal only to discover that the boys were already there.

"What are you doing here?" asked Cade, looking up from his guitar. "Coming to see how badly you're gonna lose?"

"No," said Cloe. "For your information, you're the ones who don't belong here. We reserved this space with the drama teacher."

"That's impossible," replied Cade. "So did we."

"Well, there's an easy way to settle this," said Dylan. "I'll check the sign-up sheet." He walked toward the auditorium door. "No way!" he cried after examining the schedule. "Neither of our groups is listed!"

"Let's not freak out," said Koby. "I know how to resolve this. Why don't we all use the space and rehearse together? This way, we can all get in some time practicing. Whaddya think?"

"I guess it wouldn't be so bad," said Jade. "Let's try it, but just don't get too depressed when we totally out-rock you!"

After a few minutes, everyone began to realize that apart, both bands were good, but together, they were unbelievably rockin'! When they had finished practicing the girls' song, Koby spoke up.

"Who wants to admit that we should perform together?" he asked, looking around the room.

"I will," said Jade. "Koby's right—we should have known this from the beginning."

"I'm down with bringing the two bands together," said Cade. "But on one condition."

"If your condition is that Dylan has to be our lead singer, I'm out," said Cloe, smiling.

Dylan laughed.

"I wouldn't worry about that, Angel," he said. "No one can deny that you and Sasha are the ones with the talent."

"Nah," continued Cade. "It's not that. I just think that if we come together, one of the girls should play keyboard, so Koby can help us win with amazing lighting!"

"Dude, I'll play," said Yasmin. "I can still sing backup, too."

"I have another request," said Jade. "I'd rather work on costumes than sing. You guys won't be sorry."

"That's cool, Jade," replied Cloe. "I think we'd be lucky to have you make our costumes. If there's one person in the world who's got a style that can't be beat, it's you!"

Before they knew it, the big night had arrived! Everyone was standing backstage at the Stiles High Auditorium getting ready.

"Jade," said Yasmin as she put on her costume. "You totally outdid yourself. These costumes are mad stylin'! Even if we don't win the contest, we definitely have the coolest outfits!"

"Thanks, girl," replied Jade. "With my passion for fashion, designing these costumes was majorly fun!"

As soon as the boys and girls stepped onstage, the audience knew they were in for something special. The lights dimmed. Cloe felt a rush of excitement as she looked out at all the people watching. Then the lights exploded into the spectacular display that Koby had created! The music cued, and Cloe began to sing. As soon as she finished the first verse, the audience started cheering.

Cloe smiled. *This is what I've always wanted,* she thought.

After Sasha finished her solo, the audience went nuts. Koby turned to Jade. "Wow," he said. "This is one slammin' act!"

"I know," said Jade. "There's no way we can lose! They're finishing up, so let's get ready to congratulate them!"

It was no surprise a few minutes later when the judges announced the winners—their band won!

When everyone went onstage, the audience gave them a standing ovation.

Cloe couldn't contain her excitement. "I'm so happy we won," she yelled, turning to Sasha and Cade, who were standing right next to her. "And I'm happy we came together."

"Totally," agreed Cade. "Separately, we were slammin', but together we're out of this world!"

"Yep," said Sasha, smiling at her BFFs. "And victory means more when you have awesome friends to share it with!"